eOR Rabbits

WOL

Piglet

MEET ALL THESE FRIENDS IN BUZZ BOOKS:

Thomas the Tank Engine
The Animals of Farthing Wood
Biker Mice from Mars
Fireman Sam
Joshua Jones
Rupert
Babar

First published in Great Britain 1994 by Buzz Books
an imprint of Reed Children's Books
Michelin House, 81 Fulham Road, London SW3 6RB
and Auckland, Melbourne, Singapore and Toronto.

Copyright © 1994 Michael John Brown, Peter Janson-Smith,
Roger Hugh Vaughan Charles Morgan and Timothy Michael Robinson,
Trustees of the Pooh Properties.
Published under licence from The Walt Disney Company
Adapted from Winnie-the-Pooh, first published 1926 and
The House at Pooh Corner, first published 1928.
Text by A.A. Milne and drawings by E.H. Shepard
Copyright under the Berne Convention.
Adaptation of the line illustrations and colouring by Arkadia
copyright © 1994 Reed International Books Ltd.
All rights reserved
ISBN 1 8 5591 4336
Printed in Italy

Winnie-the-Pooh and the missing tail

**From the stories by
A.A. Milne**

Eeyore stood by himself in a corner of the forest thinking about things.

Sometimes he thought sadly to himself, "Why?" and sometimes he thought, "Wherefore?" and sometimes he thought, "Inasmuch as which?" – and sometimes he didn't quite know what he *was* thinking about.

So when Winnie-the-Pooh came stumping along, Eeyore was very glad to be able to stop thinking for a little.

"Hello. How are you?" said Pooh.

Eeyore shook his head from side to side.

"Not very *how*," he said. "I don't seem to have felt at all *how* for a long time."

"Dear, dear," said Pooh. "Let's have a look at you."

Eeyore stood still and Winnie-the-Pooh walked all around him.

"What's happened to your tail?" he asked in surprise.

"What *has* happened to it?" enquired Eeyore.

"It isn't there!" said Pooh.

"Are you sure?" sighed Eeyore.

"Well, either a tail *is* there or it isn't there and yours *isn't* there!"

"Let's have a look," said Eeyore and he
turned slowly around to the place where
his tail had been a little while ago. Then,
finding that he couldn't catch it up, he
turned round the other way until he
came back to where he was at first.

At last he said, with a long, sad sigh,
"I believe you're right."

"Of course I'm right," said Pooh.

"That accounts for a good deal," said
Eeyore gloomily. "It explains everything.
No wonder."

"You must have left it somewhere," said Winnie-the-Pooh.

"Somebody must have taken it," said Eeyore. "How like them," he added, after a long silence.

Pooh felt that he ought to say something helpful about it but didn't quite know what, so he decided to do something helpful instead.

"Eeyore," he said solemnly,
"I, Winnie-the-Pooh, will find
your tail for you."

"Thank you, Pooh," answered Eeyore.
"You're a real friend," said he. "Not like
some," he said.

So Pooh went off to find Eeyore's tail.
It was a fine spring morning in the forest.
Through copse and spinney marched
Bear, down open slopes of gorse and
heather, over rocky beds of streams,
up steep banks of sandstone and into the
heather again. At last, tired and hungry,
he came to the Hundred Acre Wood.
For it was there that Owl lived.

100 AKER WOOD

"And if anyone knows anything about anything," said Bear to himself, "it's Owl," he said, "or my name's not Winnie-the-Pooh," he said. "Which it is," he added.

Owl's residence was grander than anybody else's, or seemed so to Bear, because it had both a knocker *and* a bell-pull. Underneath the knocker there was a notice which said:

PLES RING IF AN RNSER IS REQIRD.

Underneath the bell-pull there was a notice which said:

PLEZ CNOKE IF AN RNSR IS NOT REQID.

These notices had been written by
Christopher Robin, who was the only
one in the forest who could spell;
for Owl, wise though he was in many
ways, able to read and write and spell
his own name WOL, somehow went
all to pieces over delicate words like
MEASLES and BUTTERED TOAST.

Winnie-the-Pooh read the two notices
very carefully. Then he called out
in a very loud voice,
"Owl! I require an answer.
It's Bear speaking."

The door opened, and Owl looked out. "Hallo, Pooh," he said. "How's things?"

"Terrible and sad," said Pooh, "because Eeyore has lost his tail. Could you very kindly tell me how to find it for him?"

"Well," said Owl, "the thing to do is as follows. First, Issue a Reward. Then ..."

PLEZ CNOKE IF AN RNSR IS NOT REQID

"Just a moment," said Pooh holding
up his paw. "*What* do we do to this –
what you were saying? You sneezed
just as you were going to tell me."

"I *didn't* sneeze."

"Yes, you did, Owl."

"Excuse me, Pooh, I didn't. You can't sneeze without knowing it."

"Well, you can't know it without something having been sneezed."

"What I *said* was, 'First *Issue* a Reward'."

"You're doing it again," said Pooh sadly.

"A Reward!" said Owl very loudly. "We write a notice to say that we will give a large something to anybody who finds Eeyore's tail."

"I see, I see," said Pooh, nodding his head.

"Well, then," said Owl. "We write out this notice, and we put it up all over the forest."

Pooh gave a deep sigh and tried very hard to listen to what Owl was saying.

But Owl went on and on until at last he came back to where he started, and he explained that the person to write out this notice was Christopher Robin.

"Did you see the ones on my front door?"

For some time now Pooh had been saying "Yes" and "No" in turn to all that Owl was saying. He said "No, not at all," now, without really knowing what Owl was talking about.

"Didn't you see them?" said Owl, a little surprised. "Come and look at them now."

So they went outside.
And Pooh looked at the knocker
and the notice below it,
and he looked at the bell-rope
and the notice below it,
and the more he looked
at the bell-rope, the more he felt
that he had seen something like it,
somewhere else, sometime before.

PLEZ CNOKE
IF AN RNSr
IS NOT REQID

"It reminds me
of something,"
Pooh said.
"Where did
you get it?"

"I just came across it in the forest. It was hanging over a bush and I thought at first somebody lived there, so I rang it, and nothing happened and then I rang it again very loudly and it came off in my hand, and as nobody seemed to want it, I took it home, and … "

"Owl," said Pooh solemnly, "you made a mistake. Somebody did want it."

"Who?"

"Eeyore. My dear friend Eeyore. He was attached to it," said Winnie-the-Pooh sadly.

With these words
he unhooked it,
and carried it back
to Christopher Robin...

...who put it back
where it
belonged.

Eeyore frisked about the forest, waving his tail so happily that Winnie-the-Pooh came over all funny, and had to hurry home for a little snack of something to sustain him.

And, wiping his mouth half an hour
afterwards, he sang to himself proudly:

Who found the tail?
"I," said Pooh,
"At a quarter
to two (Only
it was quarter
to eleven really),
I found the tail!"

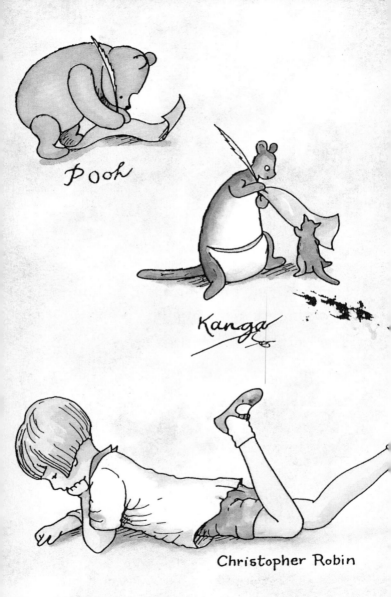

Pooh

Kanga

Christopher Robin